TOMMY'S
TRAIN RIDE
on the Alaska Railroad

ISBN 1-888125-51-9

Library of Congress
Catalog Card Number: 99-63819

Copyright 1999 by Bonnie Pennington
—First Edition—

For
Lance
and
Joseph
My
Inspiration

D1159538

Manufactured in Hong Kong

PO Box 221974 Anchorage, Alaska 99522-1974

It was a big day for Tommy. Today was his first train ride and his dad had given him his own camera for the trip.

In front of the station was a small train, almost Tommy's size. Engine #1 had been the Alaska Railroad's first engine.

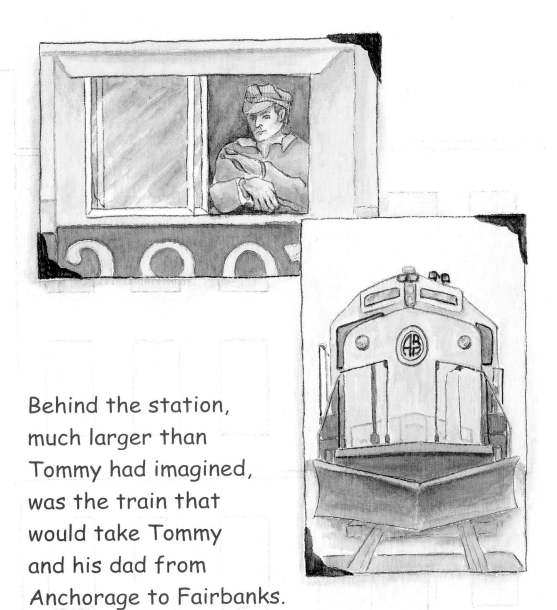

Behind the station,
much larger than
Tommy had imagined,
was the train that
would take Tommy
and his dad from
Anchorage to Fairbanks.
The engineer waved as they climbed aboard.

Over great metal bridges
and through dark tunnels,
the train made its way into
the Alaska wilderness.

It was scary, looking out the window so high above Hurricane Gulch, but Tommy was brave.

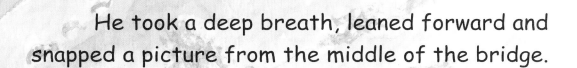

He took a deep breath, leaned forward and snapped a picture from the middle of the bridge.

They passed by mountains
so tall the tops were above
the clouds, still covered with
snow even in the summer.

Tommy saw a lot of
fishermen along the
rivers casting their
hooks for salmon.

When Tommy saw a field
blooming with fireweed,
he took a picture just for
his mom because he knew
her favorite color was pink.

Along the way,
there were lots of animals. An eagle
swooped down for a closer look and a
brown bear with her cub were searching for berries.

At one place, the train
had to stop and wait for a
bull moose to move off the tracks.

They stopped in small towns with odd names
like Talkeetna and Nenana. Tommy's dad
said that in years past,
the train brought
miners in
search of
gold. A few
lucky ones
still find a
nugget or two.

Tommy was amazed when
the train stopped without
a town in sight and a few
men hiked off into the woods.
"Hunters," his dad told him.
"The train will pick them up in a couple of days."

All too soon, it was the end of the
big day and the end of Tommy's
train ride. But Tommy still had
one picture left in his camera.

Tommy's Train Ride

"I have an idea," said his dad.
"Let's get a shot of the two of us."

This is his favorite photo.
Tommy keeps it on his dresser
with the scrapbook he made
when they got home.

The Alaska Railroad is America's only full-service railroad, offering both freight and passenger service year 'round. The route, including branch lines and sidings, covers more than 500 miles. Lines runs from tidewater at Seward to Anchorage, the state's largest city, and through the heart of Alaska to Fairbanks.

Construction of the line began in 1915 and was completed in 1923. The railroad was built in sections by work gangs. Their construction camps grew into section stations where crews who maintained the line lived with their families. Today most of the maintenance is performed by roving work crews whose families live in towns that sprang up along the tracks. Nearly 70 percent of Alaska's population lives along the railroad corridor.

The Alaska Railroad hauls a diverse load from natural resources such as coal, gravel, logs, and petroleum products, to groceries and heavy equipment. In addition, nearly 500,000 people ride the railroad every year; most are visitors to Alaska during summer.

The Alaska railroad provides a vital transportation link for rural Alaskans. There are no roads in some parts of Alaska, which

means that when some Alaskans want to come to town, travel to the railroad may involve a dog sled, all-terrain vehicle, or showmachine. Once at the tracks, rural Alaskans flag the local passenger train, which then stops to pick them up. The Alaska Railroad is the only railroad in the United States still offering this unique "flag" service.